# Harvey's Horrible
# Snake Disaster

# Eighteen Feet of Snake!

Dr. Strann turned onto the highway to the zoo. I was looking ahead, not thinking of anything special, when something like I'd never felt before moved along the back of my neck.

I was so scared, all the little fine hairs on my arms were standing at attention. I wanted to turn around and see what was there, but I just couldn't bring myself to look. All I wanted was to get away from it, whatever it was. I was starting to lean forward when Dr. Strann yelled, "Charlie!"

Charlie was loose, and Charlie was moving fast. He came slithering over the back of my seat and started winding himself around me, *all eighteen feet of him. . . .*

**Books by Eth Clifford**

The Dastardly Murder of Dirty Pete
Harvey's Horrible Snake Disaster
Harvey's Marvelous Monkey Mystery

Available from MINSTREL Books

# Harvey's Horrible Snake Disaster

by

## Eth Clifford

A MINSTREL® BOOK

PUBLISHED BY POCKET BOOKS

New York   London   Toronto   Sydney   Tokyo   Singapore

This novel is a work of fiction. Names, characters, places and incidents are either the product of the author's imagination or are used fictitiously. Any resemblance to actual events or locales or persons, living or dead, is entirely coincidental.

A Minstrel Book published by
POCKET BOOKS, a division of Simon & Schuster Inc.,
1230 Avenue of the Americas, New York, N.Y. 10020

Copyright © 1984 by Eth Clifford Rosenberg
Cover artwork copyright © 1986 by Richard Williams

Published by arrangement with Houghton Mifflin Company
Library of Congress Catalog Card Number: 83-27299

All rights reserved, including the right to reproduce this book or portions thereof in any form whatsoever.
For information address Houghton Mifflin Company,
2 Park Street, Boston, Mass. 02108

ISBN: 0-671-72957-8

First Minstrel Books printing July, 1986

10  9  8  7  6  5

A MINSTREL BOOK and colophon are trademarks
of Simon & Schuster Inc.

Printed in the U.S.A.

For Martin and Adrienne
with affection
and for our good friend
Lee M. Hoffman

# Contents

# Harvey's Horrible Snake Disaster

# 1

# In which there is much talk about snakes

"I think it's disgusting," my sister Georgeann said. "If I were a parent, I'd rather die than let my daughter do anything so disgusting."

That's the way my sister talks. My mom says it's because Georgeann is fifteen and fifteen is a very difficult age. Which is very peculiar when you think about it. Why is fifteen any worse than fourteen? Or ten going on eleven?

I'm ten, and when I say something dumb or act silly, my mom tells me to act my age.

"Harvey." She always gets that little annoyed frown right between her eyebrows. "Harvey! Will you please act your age!"

My dad doesn't care. He lets it all slide by. So when Georgeann got all dramatic one morning, he just went on spreading the jam on his toast, took a big bite, and picked up the morning paper. I think he uses it like a wall to hide behind when Georgeann starts fussing about something.

But Georgeann wasn't about to give up. "Daddy!" She flipped her long thick blond ponytail, and it went flying across her back like a whip when she tossed her head. She's just like my dad. They both have short fuses. Sometimes sparks shoot in every direction when those two get together. "You're not listening! I have to cut up a *frog*."

The way she spit out that word, you'd think she was going to slice a dinosaur. But that was just like Georgeann, complaining about probably the best thing that would happen to her all year. *We* never get to do anything that interesting in our class.

I got a sudden picture of Georgeann picking up a knife and turning her head away from the frog so she wouldn't have to see what she was doing. Even though I had problems of my own, I couldn't help grinning at her.

"What are you laughing about?" Georgeann demanded, glaring at me. She can get more fire in her eye than anybody I know, except my dad, of course. I sometimes feel sorry for the people who have to face him in traffic court.

She leaned across the table and said in that extra-sweet voice she puts on when she's going to say something rotten, "I may have to cut up a disgusting frog, but at least I don't have to look at a lot of creepy, crawly, slimy snakes."

"Snakes!" My mom clapped her hand to her face. "I'd forgotten all about the snakes. Thor," she said, turning to my dad, "please put your paper down."

She was polite, but there was a lot of iron in her "please." She's almost as tall as my dad, with black hair and eyes and what Dad calls olive skin. She's usually soft-spoken, maybe because Georgeann and my dad have lung power you wouldn't believe. When Dad gets mad he explodes; Mom turns to ice and gives everybody the silent treatment.

Dad dropped the paper just a little and peered at Mom over its edge. "Let's not go through all that again, Joy." He sounded impatient, as if snakes were all we had talked about all morning. "It's absolutely safe. Miss Platt is a fine, responsible teacher."

"Oh no she isn't." Georgeann was gloating

now. "She's going to let the kids touch them and hold them tomorrow. All those slippery snakes are going to be slithering around the room, hissing and rattling and squirming all over the place. Cutting up a frog is revolting, but at least the frog is dead," she added, looking at me meaningfully.

My stomach was beginning to turn. I once went through the snake house at the zoo and I couldn't get out of there fast enough. We went to the Crocodile Farm last year and I wasn't afraid at all, even though it made my dad uncomfortable. But there's something about snakes that makes my skin crawl.

Mom wasn't paying any more attention to Georgeann than Dad was. She said, "Georgeann, stop teasing your brother," in an absent-minded way and then went right on talking to my dad about what was really on her mind. "It's not a question of trusting Miss Platt. And I'm not worried about the snakes. It's just that Mildred and Nora are coming in on the noon plane, and I don't have to remind you how Mildred will feel if she hears about the snakes."

I groaned. I couldn't help it. I was so busy

trying to keep Georgeann from finding out how upset I was about the snakes, I'd almost forgotten about Aunt Mildred and my cousin Nora. Terrific!

"There goes my room again," Georgeann muttered under her breath. Mom heard her just the same.

"You don't hear your brother complaining about giving his room to Nora and sleeping in the living room." Mom gave Dad one of her needle-sharp glances when she said this. She's been after him for years for a bigger house, but he says we'll be grown and gone soon, so why bother. He doesn't take kindly to change.

"Your brother," my mom went on, talking to Georgeann but keeping my dad pinned to his chair with that look, "never complains about giving up his privacy."

I had a good reason for not complaining. It was a fight I never won, so I just gave up. Now I settled for giving Georgeann a noble look. I'm getting very good at it. And it drives Georgeann crazy.

She got right back at me, though. She made this awful face as if she were smelling fish ten days old. "Snakes." She wriggled her fingers in the air and whispered, "Creeping. And crawling. And *slimy.*"

I could just see hundreds of them twitching all over the classroom. I began to get goose bumps.

I didn't mind Miss Platt being creative, but why snakes? I bet there wasn't one kid in class who wasn't thinking about staying home. I'd never get away with that. But I just didn't see how I was going to get through school on snake day.

Suddenly I didn't feel too hungry anymore. I pushed my chair back a little. My dog Butch, who was watching me from the doorway, sat up and studied me. I don't know how he does it, but Butch always seems to catch on when something's bothering me. He got up right away, came over, and tried to put his head in my lap. Butch is my special pet because he and I are practically the same age.

I patted him with one hand, to thank him, and pushed him down. Then I dropped my other hand under the table. Butch's tail thumped the floor, and his cool damp nose nudged my palm. So I gave him my bacon.

"Do not feed that dog," Dad roared at me.

"You're turning him into a monster. Out," he ordered.

Butch dragged his big fat body almost to the door. Then he flopped down again and lowered his head to his outstretched paws. His eyes got sad and weepy. Sad and weepy eyes don't bother my dad. I guess he sees quite a few of those in court.

"Can we just once have a conversation without all these interruptions?" Mom hates to be sidetracked. "We were talking about the snakes."

"No we weren't," Georgeann put in helpfully. "We were talking about Aunt Mildred and her usual yearly visit."

"Young woman, I don't care for your attitude," my dad snapped at her. "You're talking about my sister. I don't think having my sister and her daughter here for two months is that difficult."

Georgeann and I looked at each other, and we had a feeling of real togetherness there for a minute.

Aunt Mildred is a tall, skinny, twitchy lady, the kind who screams and jumps if you just happen to come up behind her quietly. My dad explained that Aunt Mildred is very high-strung. To make matters worse, things just seem to happen to her. Like once when she was a kid, she stepped on some fire ants at a picnic and her feet swelled up something fierce. Another time she was at summer camp and she went swimming with a bunch of the girls. Some kid threw a snake at them. The girls screamed and laughed and carried on, but my aunt panicked and almost drowned, even though everybody told her it was just a little old harmless water snake. I have to admit, I can't blame her. I guess I would have felt the same way.

I think Aunt Mildred got in the habit of being scared, and it didn't get better as she grew up. My dad and mom get awfully impatient with her whenever she visits, but they feel sorry for her, too.

"Imagine going through life scared of your own shadow," Mom told us, trying to get us to understand my aunt a little better. They feel sorry for her. But most of all, they feel sorry for Nora.

"What that child has to put up with," Mom tells us all the time. You'd think if my mom was going to be understanding, she'd have some idea of what *I* have to put up with when my cousin Nora is around. But all she was interested in was giving us the usual yearly lecture.

"Your aunt is a very nervous person. She doesn't enjoy being so fearful about everything, but she can't help herself. That's why she won't stay in that big house of hers alone with Nora while your uncle Clarence is out of the country on business."

I sank back in my chair, waiting for the rest of it: how my uncle Clarence is some kind of special consultant who travels to South America every year, and my aunt Mildred won't go with him because she's sure the whole continent is teeming with headhunters and vampire bats and man-eating tarantulas and who knows what else. I just don't listen to all that stuff anymore.

I don't mind Aunt Mildred too much. It's my cousin Nora. Nora follows me around wherever I go. She sticks closer to me than my shadow. What's more, she asks a million questions.

And you might as well know something else about her — she's the world's biggest liar. The kids all think she's weird. Then they make fun of me for having a cousin like that.

Nobody likes it when I tell a little old fib once in a while. But when Nora lies, my mom laughs and says she is just stretching the truth. I don't think she feels that way because Nora is a guest and we have to be polite. It's probably because Nora's lies are so ridiculous.

There was the time years ago when I had to go for a blood test, and Nora wanted to come along and watch. I wasn't scared exactly, even though I was only seven then. But I wasn't real happy about it either, if you know what I mean.

Well, Nora watched that needle go into my arm, her eyes big and dark and solemn in that owl face of hers. Of course I had to make believe that I found it fascinating, too. The blood gushed out of my arm into that tube, and it felt like the tube was a mile long.

Then Nora piped up and asked the nurse to put the blood back in my arm when she was through with it. The nurse laughed and said she couldn't do that. So Nora said, "That's a waste of good blood. When I have a blood test, the nurse always makes another little hole in my arm and pours all my blood back in."

That's my cousin Nora.

While I was thinking about Nora's whopper, my mom had gone on talking to my dad. "Mildred will have a fit if she hears about the snakes," she warned him again.

He stood up. "Let's not borrow trouble, Joy."

I could see he not only didn't want to discuss it, he didn't even want to think about it. He just went tearing out of the room — he can sure move fast for a big man — leaping over Butch, who didn't even bother thumping his tail. Butch was concentrating on the table. He knew he'd be getting his scraps any second now.

"Daddy. Wait. I want a lift this morning," Georgeann shrieked after him.

I couldn't believe it. I was sure she'd come down with a case of galloping hangnails or something just so she could stay home today. "You mean, after all that carrying on about cutting up a frog, you're still going to school?" I asked.

"Why wouldn't I?" she answered calmly. "Honestly, you act like such a *child*," she said, and ran after my dad.

"I *am* a child!" I yelled. Then I remembered. Hank Clay is in her biology class.

Hank keeps slipping her notes in class. I know because I read a couple of them once when they fell out of her biology book. He writes things like, "Your eyes are like amber waves of grain." Hank Clay wouldn't know an amber wave of grain if it bit him. Anyway, Georgeann's eyes are just plain light brown, like mine.

I hope I never get that sappy about a girl.

I figured, the way Georgeann feels about Hank Clay — this term, anyway — she probably wouldn't notice if she was cutting up a frog or a baboon.

Butch didn't know whether to walk me to the bus stop or go panting into the kitchen and bark till Mom scraped the food into his dish. Like any good, smart, greedy dog, he went for the food and I took off without him.

I had a lot to think about, anyhow. On the bus, I stared out the window, but I didn't see anything. I had this feeling that just kept growing inside me.

Something would go wrong.

Something always goes wrong when my cousin Nora is around.

I was right. It started the minute I came home from school.

# 2

# In which a crystal ball foretells the future

I saw them as soon as I walked in. Aunt Mildred grabbed me and hugged me and kissed me. Then she ruffled my hair and pinched my cheek. I hate that more than anything.

Besides being scared of everything in the whole world, Aunt Mildred is a talker. She talks and talks and talks. She tells you more than you ever want to know, all the while staring at you with her big brown eyes until you feel hypnotized.

I made the mistake of asking, just to be polite, "How was your plane trip?"

Georgeann, who was standing a little behind Aunt Mildred, shook her head at me hard. But it was too late. There was no way to stop Aunt Mildred now.

14

"Our plane trip," she said with a shudder. "You just won't believe it, Harvey. It was a miracle the plane didn't drop down out of the sky. It kept making these terribly strange noises." And then she went on about a suspicious-looking couple on the plane: the man had dark eyes and a beard and kept giving the people around him wild stares, and the woman beside him kept clutching her handbag. Aunt Mildred knew at once they were hijackers.

Georgeann winked at me then and grinned. I had a hard time keeping a straight face myself.

I waited until Aunt Mildred stopped to catch her breath and I squeezed in a quick, "I'm glad to see you, too." But by then she'd already turned away from me and was jabbering to Mom, who was trying to escape into the kitchen.

Then I finally saw my cousin Nora and I could feel my jaw dropping.

"What happened to you?" I asked. I was stunned.

Last year she'd been shorter than I, and chunky, and her head seemed to sit on her body with no neck to hold it up. Now she was taller than I am by a good two inches. She still had that owl face of hers, but now there was a neck connecting it to a skinny body.

She stood there watching me, lapping it up. And then she reached over, ruffled my hair, and pinched my cheek!

"Surprised you, didn't I, Shorty."

Sure she surprised me. She's three months younger than I am. How come *she* grew and I didn't? I couldn't even depend on her staying shorter than I am.

Nora didn't wait for me to respond, just went right on talking. "Tell me, little cousin Harvey, are you wondering why I'm taller than you?"

"No," I answered. "Are you taller? I never even noticed." Then, to get even, I said, "I've got a real surprise for you, Nora." And I gave her a mean look.

Nora asked suspiciously, "What surprise?"

"You'll find out," I said. I almost felt sorry for her because I knew she'd be twice as scared as I was when she found out about the snakes.

"I can wait," she said, pretending it didn't matter. "I think I'll just go up to my room now. I hope you took all your little childish toys out."

She didn't wait for me to answer. I watched her going upstairs, my face getting hot and red because I was boiling over. *Her* room? *My* childish things? My super electronic video space games?

I went out to the sunroom to do my homework. That's where Georgeann will be sleeping for the next two months because her bedroom is too small for two people. I was so mad I did the same math problem three times without noticing what I was doing.

I simmered down by the time we sat down to supper, but I thought it wouldn't hurt to get back at Nora. So I asked my sister, "Hey, Georgeann. Did you cut up that frog today? Did you cut him up into little tiny pieces?" I was talking to Georgeann, but I was looking right at Nora.

Georgeann caught on right away. "What do you think we're having for supper?" she asked with an innocent expression.

Nora just looked me straight in the eye, but Aunt Mildred twisted the beads she was wearing and gave an uneasy little laugh.

My mom said firmly, "It's *chicken*, Mildred." Then she whipped her head around and gave me and Georgeann her old watch-it glare.

"Was that your big surprise, Harvey?" Nora asked with a superior air. "Did you think you'd scare me about having a frog for supper? You're such a silly little kid."

I was so mad at her I could feel rockets shooting off in my head. "I've got a better surprise than that," I blurted out. "Tomorrow is snake day. We're going to have snakes in the classroom. How do you like that?"

Nora didn't bat an eye, but Aunt Mildred fell back in her chair. "Snakes?" she gasped. "Live snakes?"

"Now, Mildred, it's just a nature study project." My dad made it sound as if we were going to the park to pick daisies. "Wonderful for kids. *We* never had snakes in our classrooms."

"Nora can sit right up front if she wants to," I put in helpfully, "so she can get a real good look at them."

Nora fastened her owl-stare on me. I couldn't tell what she was thinking, but I was sure she was scared. She put her napkin down, left the table, and headed upstairs. Mom and

Dad didn't pay any attention because they were busy laying down the law to Aunt Mildred. Nora was most certainly *not* going to stay home from school, not after the arguments my mom had had getting Nora into school in the first place.

"But tomorrow is Friday," my aunt protested. "She'd only miss one day."

Since my mom and dad think missing school is one of the seven deadly sins, I knew Nora would be on the school bus with me the next morning.

Georgeann was on the phone in the kitchen reading poetry — *poetry* — to Hank, so I went back to the sunroom to finish my math. I couldn't find my calculator. Dad doesn't usually let me use it when I'm doing homework. I felt I'd already had a hard enough day, though, so I went upstairs to get it from my desk.

When I got to the door of my room, the idea of getting the calculator flew right out of my mind. Nora was standing in front of the dresser, studying herself in the mirror. She had a red scarf wrapped around her head like a turban; my mom's long gold earrings were dangling from her ears. She'd drawn black lines

19

straight across her thick eyebrows and down around her eyes with Mom's eyebrow pencil.

"What do you think you're doing?" I yelled. "My mom will kill you. She hates people using her things."

Nora turned around, raised one hand, and waved me into the room with a long, slow gesture.

"Enter," she said in a deep voice.

I stared at her. She was acting like someone in a weird TV show. She sure had changed since last year. I didn't know from one minute to the next now what she was going to do or say.

She sat down on my bed, reached under the pillow, and pulled out the crystal ball George-ann had given me. It was a prop she'd used when she had a part as a gypsy fortune teller in last year's school play.

"Hey! That's mine." I started to object, but Nora shook her head and put her finger against her lips.

"Silence." She peered down, made a circle with her hand over the crystal, and frowned. "I can see your future."

20

I pushed next to her on the bed and looked for myself. "No, you can't. It's just a dumb old piece of glass."

She gave me a mysterious look. "Only those with the power can see," she told me in a spooky voice. "Many strange and terrible things will happen to you. Danger! I see danger! Beware the snakes!" She covered the ball with her hand.

"You have been warned." She spaced the words out slowly. Then she closed her eyes, let the ball roll out of her hand, and fell back on the bed.

I knew it was all a big act, but she made me nervous anyway. Still, I wasn't going to let her know that. So I caught the ball before it rolled off the bed and made a horrible moaning sound. Nora half-opened one eye to see what I was up to. I looked down into the ball, staggered back, grabbed my throat and croaked, "It's true. I can see the future, too. I see you disappearing."

Nora sat up and looked at me thoughtfully. Too thoughtfully, almost as if she was tossing an idea back and forth in her mind.

Well, I wasn't going to hang around waiting

to find out. I tossed the ball back onto the bed, picked up the calculator from my desk, and got as far as the door when Nora spoke.

"Harvey," she whispered, sounding real creepy. "All things predicted in the glass will come to pass. Remember that when day breaks."

"Terrific," I told her, and went downstairs to finish my homework.

I forgot every word she said until the next morning, when I woke up and Nora was missing.

She had disappeared.

# 3
# In which a dog finds a missing girl

Aunt Mildred found out first. She came tearing into the kitchen, yelling, "She's gone. She's been kidnaped. My baby's been kidnaped. Call the police. Get the FBI."

She didn't know whether to cry or run around in circles, so she did both.

"Mildred!" Dad clutched his head. "We can't hear ourselves think. Must you be so hysterical?"

"Only two months to go," my sister muttered to Mom, "less one day."

"Mildred," my mom said. "Sit down and have some coffee. Nora is not a baby. She's ten years old. There's probably a perfectly reasonable explanation . . ."

"I have been all around the house and the

23

yard, Joy. I've been up and down the street. I tell you she's gone. She just vanished."

So that's what Nora was hinting at last night when she was holding the crystal ball, I told myself. She was planning to disappear. I didn't know what to do. If I mentioned the conversation Nora and I had had, they'd start blaming me for sure.

Just then Butch came in, barking and racing back and forth and barking again.

My dad hates turmoil at the breakfast table. He was trying hard to control his temper and not argue with his sister on the very first morning of her visit. So he just flashed her a furious glance and turned on Butch.

"OUT!"

Butch started to slink out, but Georgeann called him back. While she petted him, Butch gave her his most loving look, licked her hand, and made a crying sound.

I'd never get away with that kind of act, calling Butch back after my dad threw him out. But he lets Georgeann do practically anything.

"He's trying to tell us something. He wants us to follow him," I said.

Butch must have known I was talking about

him because he started to bark again. Between Aunt Mildred's babbling and Butch's carrying-on there was so much commotion, we all agreed it would be easier to see where Butch would take us. So we piled out of the kitchen into the back yard, where Butch raced to the big oak tree, backed up a little, raised his head, and howled up into the air.

"What is it? What does he want?" Aunt Mildred asked. "I don't see anything."

Just then a squirrel skittered across a branch, ran down the tree, and took off across the yard with Butch loping after him.

"Dogs!" Aunt Mildred was angry. "All that commotion about a squirrel."

But I'd been studying the tree.

"Hey!" I pointed up to one of the higher branches. "Look."

Now they could all see what I had spotted, a blue and white sneaker peeking out between the leaves.

"Nora!" Aunt Mildred sobbed with relief.

"NORA!" They must have heard my dad in the next county. "Nora Jean Adams, you come down out of that tree this minute." The way he roared, I was surprised the sound alone didn't knock Nora loose from her perch. It sure got some action.

The leaves rustled, a couple of branches parted, and there was Nora, peering down at us.

"Thor. Please," Aunt Mildred begged. "Go up and bring her down. She can't manage alone."

"She got up there without help, didn't she?" My dad's voice was sharp. "Down!" he ordered Nora.

Butch, who had lost the squirrel and come back, stretched out full length at once. At least *he* recognized a command when he heard one.

"I won't come down unless I don't have to go to school," Nora called. "And if anybody tries to make me go to school, I'll jump."

"How dare you try to blackmail us?" My dad has this very fair skin that goes with his white-blond hair and his piercing blue eyes. Just then that fair skin turned so red, it looked as if it had been dipped in beet juice.

I began to wonder what Nora's real reason was for not wanting to go to school. I didn't think it was only because of the snakes. Maybe she knew that a lot of the kids thought she was kind of weird.

Mom decided it was time to step in and take charge of the situation.

"Thor," she said, "will you hold back the thunderbolts for a while? Nora. Get down here at once or you'll miss the school bus. This whole thing is just too ridiculous," she went on impatiently. "We went to a lot of trouble to get you registered for class. There's no reason for you to stay home today. I promise you that Harvey will see that nothing happens to you. Isn't that right, Harvey?"

The way Mom was looking at me, I knew I'd better promise in a hurry, so I did.

I promised to take care of Nora, but I never promised I'd talk to her. I didn't say one word to her on the bus. She didn't seem to want to talk, anyway. She just sat there staring at nothing with a fixed look. Her lips were set in a straight line and she was scowling.

All of a sudden she whipped around and caught me studying her. "You got a problem, Harvey?" she asked in an angry voice.

I just shrugged, turned my head away,

opened one of my books, and made believe I was studying. To get my attention again, I guess, she began to whistle. She didn't even know how to pucker her lips last year, and now she was whistling! I even recognized the tune. She was almost as good as I am, and I'm pretty good.

When she saw the expression on my face, she stopped whistling long enough to give me one of her superior smiles. Then she started whistling again.

I shut my eyes and tried to imagine her stuck in the middle of a snake pit, with snakes slithering and climbing all around her.

"Save me! Save me!" Nora was begging me.

I stood at the edge of the pit, listening to her pleading.

"You promise never to ruffle my hair again? Or pinch my cheeks?"

"I promise. Please, Harvey."

"Or ever tell another whopper?"

"Harvey," she wailed, "I'll do anything you say."

By the time we got to school, I had a smile on my face, too.

# 4
# In which macaroni solves a problem

The minute we stepped down from the bus, Nora began to drag her feet. She stopped to pick a leaf off one of the bushes, examining it as if she'd just wandered in from a desert and had never seen anything green before.

I kept hurrying her along until we finally got as far as my classroom. Outside the door, Nora hesitated.

"You go ahead, Harvey," she told me. "I have to get a drink of water."

"I'll go with you," I said promptly. Mom had made me responsible for Nora, and I wasn't going to take any chances that she'd do another disappearing act.

"Never mind. I'm not thirsty anymore," she said in a grouchy voice. "Let's get this over with." She took a deep breath and plunged into the room like someone diving into a pool of ice water.

Every head swiveled around. Nora's feet promptly took root. She couldn't seem to get her legs moving. She stared at the class, and the class stared back.

I could see Don Lopez on the right nudging Pete Warren in front of him, and Pete rolling his eyes around, letting his tongue hang out at the corner of his mouth, both of them making sure Nora saw them. Alongside them, in the next row, Candy Brinker was sitting and staring up at the ceiling, sighing and making faces, as if the sight of Nora was more than she could stand.

Nora got a little pale and swallowed hard. That's when I knew for sure that it wasn't the snakes that had Nora so upset about coming to school. It was the kids — especially Don and Pete and Candy — that bothered her.

Miss Platt leaped right in with a warm smile. She put her arm around Nora and kind of propelled her farther into the room.

"Class, I want you to welcome Nora Jean Adams."

Miss Platt is the kind of teacher who keeps things humming along. Before Nora knew what was happening, she was sitting next to me in the back of the room, and we got right into our reading assignment. After that, Nora seemed to relax.

But when lunchtime came, I practically had to shove her into the cafeteria. We got through the line without any problems and I thought everything would work out all right. The only two seats left, though, were at the table where Don and Pete and Candy were sitting. They saw us coming, so of course they started whispering and giggling and giving us the kind of looks kids give you when they want you to know they're making fun of you.

Nora hesitated for a minute, then she seemed to make up her mind about something. She started to walk by Candy with her head up high, but Candy said, making sure everybody around her could hear, "Well, look who's back, Nora the Borer, queen of the big-time liars. We really *missed* her, didn't we?"

Nora turned around, looked down at Candy, and slowly tipped her macaroni and cheese into Candy's lap. Candy jumped up and started to say something nasty, but then she caught the look in Nora's eye.

"The next guy who says something to me I don't like will get a *bath* in this stuff," Nora announced.

Candy stepped back in a hurry, and even Don and Pete seemed uneasy. Nora looked and sounded as though she'd keep her promise.

We took our seats and Nora acted as if nothing had happened.

We had the quietest table in the cafeteria after that. The others got up and left, and Nora wasn't interested in talking at all. When the bell rang, we went back to class. I figured we'd be doing math now, same as we always do. But the herpetologist came a little early, and Miss Platt didn't want to keep him waiting.

She called the class to order, waited for the whispering to die down, and said, "Now, boys and girls, at last! The moment we've all been waiting for, the chance to observe snakes at first hand."

She beamed. Miss Platt always beams when she feels she's giving us something special to think about.

"Let's welcome Dr. Benjamin Strann. Dr.

Strann, as I explained the other day, is a herpetologist."

"A herpetologist is a specialist in reptiles," I
whispered to Nora. "He's — "

"I know that. Everybody knows that," she
said.

Well *I* didn't know until Miss Platt told us.
That was something else about Nora. Last year
she was always after me to explain this or that,
but now I couldn't tell her anything.

"We have millions of snakes in California,"
she was saying. "We even eat rattlesnake sand-
wiches for breakfast."

I guess she didn't realize how loud her voice
was. Pete and Don began to snicker. Nora just
gritted her teeth and buried her head in one of
the books on her desk. I could feel my face
getting hot and flushed.

Luckily Miss Platt rapped her knuckles on
her desk and called the class to order sharply.
Then our guest appeared.

I don't know what herpetologists are supposed to look like, but Dr. Strann sure surprised me. His thick black hair was all ruffled.
He had big broad shoulders that were squared
away in a T-shirt that read: HAVE YOU

HUGGED A SNAKE TODAY? He seemed like a football player who'd just come off the field after practice.

"All right," he said. "Let's talk snakes. And let's look at snakes, right up close. Before we get started, though, I want you to know you're all absolutely safe. So if you're worried or scared, forget it. I want you all to enjoy our time together. Okay?"

Enjoy? What did he mean, enjoy? How do you *enjoy* snakes?

It looked as if he'd brought all the snakes in the world to our class, the way he began dipping into the cages and bringing them out one by one. There was the garter snake, the hognose snake, the hoop snake, the milk snake, and more that I don't remember.

Maybe it was the way Dr. Strann was handling the snakes and even stroking them once in a while, or all the different things he kept telling us, but all of a sudden I realized I'd never once had a creepy, crawly sensation. I never once felt the way I had in the snake house.

I wasn't wild about learning how snakes swallow their prey whole. But it *was* interesting to find out that snakes don't have ears. They can sense sound, Dr. Strann explained, through vibrations in the ground. The one thing that got to me most, though, was that snakes sleep with their eyes open because they don't have movable eyelids.

I'd been paying close attention to Dr. Strann, but then Nora did something that really distracted me. She leaned back in her seat, forcing her eyes open as wide as she could.

"What are you *doing?*" I whispered, but I wanted to yell. I was afraid somebody would turn around and see how peculiar she looked.

"I'm pretending to sleep like a snake to see how it feels. You ought to try it."

Everybody was facing front, so I did try. I had to quit after a couple of minutes because I began to get glassy-eyed and dizzy.

"I wonder how snakes do that," Nora said.

"I don't care how they do it. If snakes want to sleep that way, that's fine with me."

"Shhh," Nora said. "I can't hear what Dr. Strann is saying."

What Dr. Strann was saying was that snakes are our friends. He smiled at us. "I can see from your faces that you don't believe me.

Well, let me ask you something. How would you feel about rats and mice getting into your house and eating your food?"

"Yuch!" Candy Brinker called out. "That's revolting."

"One pair of mice," Dr. Strann went on, "could breed more than a million offspring in just one year if snakes weren't around to eat them."

If Georgeann thought one dead frog was disgusting, I wondered what she would say about a million mice.

"One farming community decided to get rid of its snakes. The rats took over. They ran wild. They destroyed the crops. They even ate most of the chickens."

I raised my hand. "Snakes are good for getting rid of rats, I guess. But they aren't good for people. They're poisonous, and they bite," I told him.

"*Some* snakes are poisonous," Dr. Strann corrected. "Would it surprise you to learn that the harmless snakes often make good pets?"

It surprised me, all right.

Dr. Strann began counting off on his fingers all the good reasons snakes make such great pets. "They don't have to be fed very often. You don't have to put them in a kennel when you go away from the house for a time."

I had to choke back a laugh, just picturing taking a snake to a kennel. That would be some sight, wouldn't it? Putting snakes in with all those cats and dogs?

Dr. Strann was still counting. "Snakes are quiet. They're clean. And you never have to walk a snake, either."

I sat back in my seat and kind of day-dreamed, missing a whole lot more stuff about snakes. I was just trying to imagine myself putting a leash on a snake and taking it for a walk in the neighborhood. Butch would go crazy! Aunt Mildred would pack up and go home. And she'd take Nora with her!

I began to feel more friendly toward snakes.

I must have missed a lot, because one of the kids was complaining, "But snakes are so ugly."

"Ugly?" You'd think Dr. Strann had never heard the word before. "Ugly?"

He reached into one of the cages and lifted the snake he took out up high so we could see it clearly.

"This is an Arizona Ridgenose rattlesnake, usually highly dangerous and poisonous. Because we use it in our demonstrations, this snake has been made harmless by removing its fangs and venom glands. You wouldn't call this snake ugly, would you? Just look at its colors and design."

He turned away from us for a minute and picked something up from Miss Platt's desk. When he turned around again, his face was covered by a mask.

"This is the way an Apache warrior looked with his war paint on. All the markings and colors and design were copied from the Ridgenose."

Nora jumped up. "That's beautiful! That design would be terrific printed on a dress. Or anything." I never saw Nora so enthusiastic before.

"Good for you," Dr. Strann told her. "You see, boys and girls, how nature can stretch our imaginations?"

He put the snake back in the cage. Then he gave us a big bright smile, as if he had a treat for us.

"Okay. I've told you snakes are our friends.

Now I'd like you to meet a good friend of mine. I want you to meet Charlie."

He reached into another cage. When he took this snake out, we all gasped.

Charlie had to be the longest, biggest snake in the whole world. He had the coldest, meanest-looking eyes I ever saw. The way his long tongue kept darting in and out of his mouth made us shiver.

Some of the kids sitting in front of the room jumped up out of their seats and moved back. Even Miss Platt seemed nervous.

What Charlie did next made me lose any good feelings I might have gotten about snakes from Dr. Strann's talk.

That enormous snake began to wind himself around and around Dr. Strann!

Charlie didn't look like anybody's friend. Not like anybody's friend at all. I was positive that Nora was probably ready to faint.

But I was wrong.

Nora was absolutely spellbound!

# 5
# In which an 18-foot friend is introduced

"This magnificent creature is an Indian python." Dr. Strann didn't seem to mind being squeezed by good old Charlie. "Right now he weighs a hundred and fifty pounds and is about eighteen feet long." Dr. Strann laughed. "It's hard to measure the length of a snake, especially one this size."

I could see how it would be. Who'd want to grab a snake like Charlie and stretch him out straight?

Just then Nora leaned forward. She was practically sitting on the edge of her seat. Her eyes seemed to have gotten bigger and darker and shinier.

"Isn't he beautiful?" she said, kind of catching her breath.

I looked at Charlie again and shook my head. Beautiful? He wasn't beautiful. He was a monster. Nora was just one surprise after another.

All of a sudden she jumped up and called out, "Please. Could I touch him? Could I see what he feels like?"

The way Dr. Strann lit up, you'd think Nora had just given him a present.

"Good for you, young lady," he said. "Come right along."

Miss Platt was all smiles, too.

I couldn't sit still for that. There was no way I could let Nora go up there by herself with the whole class watching. I had to seem at least as brave as she was. So I jumped up and called out, "That's just what I was going to ask."

I didn't wait for an answer, just rushed up to Dr. Strann. Nora tried to get ahead of me, but I got there first. Still, she managed to put her hand on Charlie at the same time I did. I noticed nobody else in the class was in a hurry to join us.

"Well?" Dr. Strann asked us after a minute or two.

I had to admit that Charlie felt a lot better than I expected — dry and smooth and kind of

41

pleasant. And warm, too. So much for all the things Georgeann said about snakes. What did she know?

"You thought he'd be slimy," Dr. Strann said, watching my face.

"I didn't say that. My sister did," I said, defending myself.

Dr. Strann nodded. "People have a lot of mistaken notions about snakes."

"He feels like the leather chair in my father's office," Nora said. "Hey! I can feel his muscles moving under his skin." She couldn't seem to stop stroking Charlie.

Miss Platt wanted everybody in the class to come up and touch the python. I could see that Candy Brinker hated the whole idea, but she couldn't let Nora show her up. So she stuck her hand out kind of gingerly, gave a quick giggle, then snatched it back. Pete really stroked Charlie, but his heart wasn't in it, and he was glad when Don pushed him out of the way. Don held his breath at first, but after a minute he began to enjoy it, looking around at the kids and saying, "This is great."

Once the rest of the class saw how safe it was, they got brave and crowded close. When

Charlie suddenly changed his position, though, they jumped back and Candy screamed. I almost jumped back myself until I caught Nora looking at me as if she expected me to.

After a while Miss Platt made us all sit down again, and Dr. Strann put Charlie back in his cage. Snake day had turned out to be so interesting, I was almost sorry when Dr. Strann said, "And this finishes the demonstration, boys and girls."

Nora started to clap her hands, so the rest of us did, too. Dr. Strann gave us another broad, pleased smile.

"Can I get a couple of volunteers to help me take the cages out to my car?" he asked Miss Platt.

Nora was up and moving to the front of the room almost before he got the words out.

"I'll help. I'm strong. Please, can I?" she asked.

So I had no choice again. I gave Nora a dirty look when I got close, but it didn't bother her one little bit.

"Will they have time to assist you and still catch their bus?" Miss Platt wanted to know.

"No problem," Dr. Strann replied. "I'll be

glad to give them a ride home. But maybe you'd better call their mothers and let them know Harvey and Nora will be a little late getting home."

Aunt Mildred wasn't going to like our coming home late. She'd start thinking of all the things that could happen before we got there; she'd probably drive Mom out of her mind. Then Mom would get mad at me. She'd tell me I had no right to volunteer, knowing the way my aunt would carry on. Right now, I didn't care, though, because I could see the other kids thought I was awfully brave.

That part was worth it. Even so, the last thing I wanted to do was get into a car full of snakes. The idea of being that close to them made me feel crawly again. But I was trapped, another thing I had Nora to thank for.

Dr. Strann's car turned out to be a small van. I threw my books and gym bag on the floor in front before we handed the cages to him. He set them up in the back and then waved us in. Nora hopped right in next to the cages. I hesitated. Nora didn't notice the way I held back. Dr. Strann did, though.

"Harvey, look." He reached into the van,

pulled out a small cage, and removed a black snake with a greenish-yellow color underneath. "You remember Slider, don't you?"

Nora, who was hanging out the window, said, "You showed us Slider in class. Isn't he the one you said didn't belong to the zoo? He's your own personal pet, right?"

Dr. Strann nodded. "Good girl. You remembered."

Nora beamed and gave me a smug look.

"He's the hognose snake, the one with the ugly nose," I said. I guess that showed Nora I was just as smart as she was.

"Excellent, Harvey. Excellent. Except it's called a snout. The snout makes it possible for the hognose to burrow under the ground. People who don't know the hognose sometimes mistake it for a rattlesnake."

"Why?" Nora wanted to know. She wanted Dr. Strann to tell us again, even though he had explained it in class.

"When the hognose is frightened, it puffs up its head, flattens its back, and blows and hisses — quite a loud hissing noise."

"And then it attacks."

Dr. Strann shook his head. "No, Harvey.

Don't you remember? It only pretends to be vicious. If the hissing doesn't work, and the hognose is still alarmed, it just rolls over on its back and plays dead."

"Isn't that clever!" Nora exclaimed.

For once I had to agree with her.

Dr. Strann insisted that we pet Slider. He said touching Slider would help us overcome some of our fear.

Nora really took to Slider, maybe because he was small, only about eighteen inches long. She began to talk to him softly, just as if Slider were any old regular soft pet. Still, when Dr. Strann decided it was time to put Slider back in his cage, he let me do it, and not Nora.

When we started to drive off, Dr. Strann said, "I'd like to run the snakes back to the zoo as long as your folks know you'll be late coming home. If you don't mind, of course."

Nora leaned forward and said, "I'd like a snake like Slider for a pet. Can I get one from you?"

"If your parents consent," he told her, "I can help you. But I have to warn you that a lot of parents aren't too keen about having a snake in the house."

"You don't know my mother," she said, and looked him right in the eye without blinking. "She's used to animals. See, my father is a lion tamer in a circus."

I shook my head. Didn't she ever stop? "Does he take his glasses off before he sticks his head in their mouths?" I asked sarcastically.

You know what she said? She told me not to be silly! Those were her exact words.

"Don't be silly, Harvey. My father wears contact lenses. Of course, sometimes they fall out," she went on, sounding very honest and sincere.

I was glad when she finally stopped talking, even though Dr. Strann was smiling. She really embarrassed me.

In a few minutes, Dr. Strann turned onto the highway to the zoo. I was looking ahead, not thinking of anything special, when all of a sudden Nora gasped. At the same time, something like I'd never felt before moved along the back of my neck.

I was so scared, all the little fine hairs on my arms were standing at attention. I wanted to turn around and see what was there, but I just couldn't bring myself to look. All I wanted was to get away from it, whatever it was. I was starting to lean forward when Dr. Strann yelled, "Charlie!"

Charlie was loose, and Charlie was moving fast. He came slithering over the back of my seat and started winding himself around me, *all eighteen feet of him*.

I wanted to faint, but I didn't know how.

Charlie kept on going. While the bottom part of Charlie had me tied up, the upper part was sliding along the seat and beginning to coil around Dr. Strann.

There was a hundred and fifty pounds of python fighting us for space up front.

I was scared out of my mind.

We're all going to die, I thought.

# 6

# In which almost all is lost

I took a deep breath and opened my mouth wide to yell my head off. Who had a better right? Suppose you found yourself sitting up front in a car, minding your own business, and all of a sudden tons of snake wrapped himself around you. What would you do? Say something polite, like, "Excuse me, Charlie, but I was here first?"

Anyway, it didn't matter what I planned to do, because before I could get started, Dr. Strann said in a quick, sharp, but quiet voice, "Be absolutely still, Harvey. Don't frighten him. He's very nervous."

*Charlie* was nervous? Here I had almost dropped dead from shock, and this guy was worried about his crazy snake! And while he was warning me not to upset good old Charlie, Dr. Strann was zigzagging down the highway, trying to drive with one hand and wrestle Charlie with the other.

"Pull off the road! Pull off the road!" I yelled. I was turning green. Dr. Strann's driving was scaring me almost as much as the python.

"You're so dumb, Harvey," Nora said in my ear. She was leaning over the back of my seat. For the first time I noticed that she was pushing and pulling at Charlie, digging her hands into his body to make him let go of me. "Can't you see how Charlie has wrapped himself around Dr. Strann's legs? His foot is jammed against the gas pedal. He can't pull off the road if he can't stop speeding. And he can't stop speeding if he can't put a foot on the brake."

Cars were blaring their horns at us. One woman even shouted out her car window and shook her fist in the air.

I will say for Nora, even though I hate to admit it, that she didn't seem to be going to pieces. I wouldn't have been a bundle of nerves either if I had been behind Charlie the way she was instead of being slowly squeezed like a ripe banana by a snake who didn't know when to quit.

Finally Nora must have done something right, because all at once Charlie let go of me and really concentrated on Dr. Strann. He wrapped himself around his owner as if he were trying him on for size.

I was so relieved I just sat there taking in big gulps of air.

I turned around to see if Nora was all right. Just as I did, Nora's eyes got big and scared. She sucked in her breath and then let out a screech that shook my hair loose from its roots. I figured she'd finally gone out of her mind from shock, because she was pointing and gibbering and I swear it sounded like she was saying, "Turkey! Turkey!"

I could think of a lot of names to call Charlie, but Turkey wasn't one of them. Since Nora was still pointing, I swung around and stared out the front window.

Straight ahead, a huge truck was jackknifed clear across both lanes. Crates had spilled out of the back of the truck and broken open, and what looked like a million turkeys were running around, gobbling and getting in each other's way.

The truck driver was out on the road, yelling at them, waving his arms, trying to shoo them back to the truck. A bunch of people, who had pulled over farther up the road, were racing around, laughing, chasing the turkeys as though it were some new kind of game.

I knew we were going to smash into that truck. The last thing I would ever see in this world would be those stupid gobblers.

Nora's blast when she saw the turkeys did more than just paralyze me. The vibrations from her shout drove old Charlie batty. He let go of Dr. Strann and headed for the back of the car as if he were being chased by a war party.

Nora saw him coming and flipped up the lid of his cage fast. Charlie slid in and flattened himself against the back of the cage as if he couldn't get far enough away from all of us peculiar humans. Nora slammed the lid down and latched it almost before Charlie had wiggled his whole body in.

Meanwhile, Dr. Strann slammed on the brakes, sliding to a stop off the side of the road just inches away from the truck. Then he just sat there, holding on to the wheel, not saying a word. He didn't even look up when the turkeys surrounded us, pecking at the van with their beaks, shaking their ugly red wattles at us, gobbling away like crazy.

Nora pulled away from the side window, trembling, shrinking back against her seat with her hands hugging her elbows close to her body as if she had a chill. I suddenly realized that while Nora wasn't bothered one little bit by snakes, she was sure chickenhearted when it came to turkeys. Before I could say anything, we heard a siren wailing and saw lights spinning around on a car coming up quickly. It stopped beside us, and two policemen got out. While one walked over to talk to the truck driver, the other came over to the van. He was hopping mad. He had to shove quite a few turkeys out of the way, and that didn't improve his temper any.

He invited Dr. Strann to step out of the car. Then he asked him to open his wallet and remove his driver's license.

Dr. Strann tried to explain. The policeman listened, then leaned through the window and studied the inside of the van. Of course, all he could see was me sitting in the front, hardly able to move a muscle after what we'd just been through, and Nora hunched up in the back, looking pale, and a lot of quiet snakes in cages.

The policeman walked to the back of the van and peered in. All the cages were locked.

"You're telling me," he said, walking back to Dr. Strann, "that one of the snakes — "

"The python." Dr. Strann nodded.

" — this python unlatched his cage, got into the front of the car and tried to drive it, and then just conveniently hopped in back and locked himself up again in his cage? A real obliging snake . . ."

Dr. Strann shook his head. I could see he thought it was hopeless, but he tried again, anyway. "Officer. You're not really getting the picture at all. Let me explain."

The officer held up his hand as though he were stopping traffic. "Hey, listen pal," he said. "Don't explain it to me. Just tell it to the judge."

# 7

# In which we meet the Fire-Eater himself

You know how sometimes a day starts off rotten, and you think it can't get any worse, but it does? I thought that I'd hit rock bottom when Charlie started driving the van. But I didn't know what rock bottom was until we were marched into the courtroom and there was my dad, good old Judge Willson the Fire-Eater himself, sitting on the bench. It's not a bench at all, just kind of a big desk, but that's what they call it.

When my dad caught sight of me and Nora, he was stunned. But he was in the middle of listening to an argument from some speeder, so he had to keep on paying careful attention to what the woman was telling him.

Dad was wearing a black robe. Traffic

judges don't have to; they can just wear regular suits. But my dad wants speeders to respect the law. He wants them to remember him when they get behind the wheels of their cars again. He says that black robe makes an impression. It certainly made one on me. I could see that even Nora was overwhelmed.

Sitting up there, higher than anybody else in the room, looking like the Avenger of the Road, my dad was a different man — lots bigger, somehow.

When it was our turn, the arresting officer explained how Dr. Strann had been tearing down the highway. My dad hung on every word, his face getting red and his eyes crackling with fury.

When the officer was finally finished, there was a long minute of silence. Dr. Strann must have been wondering if it was safe to try to defend himself with my dad glaring at him and his knuckles bone-white from holding his gavel so tightly.

"Well, Doctor," Dad said at last in the coldest voice you ever heard, "what are you waiting for? I assume you've prepared a reasonable explanation for all this, including why you endangered the lives of my son and niece."

"Your son and niece?" Dr. Strann swallowed hard. I thought he was going to forget about trying to explain, but he gulped and plunged right in with his side of the story.

"Your Honor, I'm a herpetologist." He pointed to the cages of snakes that the officer had brought in as evidence. The snakes were curled up inside, some of them resting their heads against the wire mesh that kept them enclosed. "I gave a demonstration in a classroom today, and these young people volunteered . . . your son and niece, I mean. Your Honor, I didn't know who they were —"

"Get on with it," Dad made the words sound as if they were being cracked out with a whip.

I felt sorry for Dr. Strann. His day was turning out to be as rotten as mine.

"Uncle Thor," Nora spoke up suddenly. "It wasn't Dr. Strann's fault. I can tell you what happened. Charlie — that's the python — got loose and slid up front and wrapped himself around Dr. Strann. Then Charlie took over the car and made it go faster and —"

"NORA!"

Dad's roar stopped her cold.

He didn't believe her! The one time in her life she'd actually told the truth, and he didn't believe her!

"Dad," I said, "it's true. What happened was —"

"I'll deal with you later, young man," he told me.

I don't argue with my dad when he calls me "young man" in that voice.

He turned to Dr. Strann again. "Knowing that you were transporting dangerous animals, you nonetheless took two young children in your van, exposing them to —"

"I assure you," Dr. Strann broke in, "the snakes were securely locked in their cages."

"Then how did the python get loose?" Dad asked acidly.

I could tell that that question stopped Dr. Strann in his tracks. He'd been so busy fighting Charlie, and later explaining to the policeman, and now defending himself in court, I suppose he hadn't had time to figure that one out yet.

"I don't know." Dr. Strann shook his head. "It beats me. I have never had a snake escape from a cage in all the years I've been giving demonstrations at schools."

I stole a look at Nora. She had the strangest expression on her face.

"You checked the cages when you took them from the classroom?" Dad wanted to know.

"Of course I did. Do you think I'm some kind of fool?" Dr. Strann's temper was beginning to rise. "I tell you they were locked."

"No sir," Dad contradicted him. "They were not. I tell *you* that your fabrication about the python does not sit well with this court."

"Uncle Thor," Nora said. It came out as a sort of croak.

"Be quiet, Nora."

"Uncle Thor. I opened the cage."

My dad swung around and stared down at her.

"You did *what?*"

"It's not the way it sounds," Nora said, her voice nervous and quick. "I just wanted to stroke him, that's all. I knew I'd never get another chance once he was back in the zoo."

She hesitated for a second, as if she was deciding whether or not she could confide in him.

Then she continued, "I wanted to tell him that I liked him. I know snakes don't have ears, but I thought Charlie would understand just from the sound of my voice."

She looked away from my dad then and said, so quietly we almost didn't hear her, "I felt sorry for him. It's lonely when nobody likes you."

Dad cleared his throat. Then he asked, gently, so Nora would know he wasn't scolding but just wanted to know, "Didn't you realize what would happen when you opened the cage?"

She shook her head. "I didn't know how much Charlie wanted to be free. I didn't know he could move that fast."

Dr. Strann had wheeled around when Nora began explaining. "I don't know what to say. Nothing like this has ever happened to me before," he muttered.

"I didn't think there was any harm in it. You told us he was perfectly safe. You said Charlie was our friend."

Dr. Strann clutched the sides of his head with both hands.

"She opened the cage." He couldn't get over it. "She let him out in a moving car." He looked up at my dad, dropped his hands to his side, and shook his head in disbelief.

Dad wasn't going to let go; he was used to all kinds of wild explanations.

"It doesn't excuse your driving like a maniac," he insisted.

Dr. Strann's temper rose a little higher. "Have you ever seen a python up close, Your Honor? No? Then I think it's time you met Charlie."

Dr. Strann walked over to Charlie's cage, reached in, let Charlie wind himself around and around, and got as close to my dad as he could.

Dad isn't afraid of much, but he couldn't help rocking back in his chair.

"I'm convinced," he said hastily. "I see your point. Case dismissed."

Dr. Strann put Charlie back in his cage. Dad told him an officer would help take all the cages out to his van. He also advised Dr. Strann to get us home as quickly as possible, and he made sure that Nora understood there was to be no funny stuff in the van.

Dr. Strann had calmed down some by the time we got back to the van, but he was still simmering a little. I guess that's why he said in a cold voice, "I want you to sit up front, Nora, where I can keep an eye on you."

Nora got into the van without a word. She just sat down in front, propped her feet up on my books, settled my gym bag on the floor against the door, and stared straight ahead.

I got in back with all the cages. I wasn't happy about that, but I figured the worst that could happen had already happened. All I had to do was edge forward on the seat and pretend the snakes weren't there.

"You can give me my books and gym bag," I started to tell Nora, but Dr. Strann interrupted. "Just leave them where they are," he snapped. "They're not in her way, and I'd like to get started."

Tears began to stream down Nora's face. "I'm sorry, Dr. Strann. I know you're mad at me. I don't blame you. I just never stopped to think — " She broke off and rubbed her face with the back of her hand.

"Don't do that, Nora. There's no need to

cry." Dr. Strann was uncomfortable. "Listen. I'm not all that angry anymore."

"You're not?" Nora's face brightened. "You mean it?"

Dr. Strann didn't answer; he just nodded and put the key into the ignition.

"Then before we go, could I ask a favor?"

Dr. Strann turned around and stared at Nora suspiciously. "What kind of a favor?"

Nora kept her voice so low, I almost missed what she was saying. "I won't ever get a chance again. Not ever."

Dr. Strann studied her. "Whatever it is, I have a feeling the answer is no."

"I just wanted to know if I could hold Slider for a while. In his cage," she added in a hurry. "Please, Dr. Strann. My mom will never let me have a snake. I won't hurt him. I just want to hold the cage and look at him."

Dr. Strann sighed, shook his head, and muttered something under his breath. He jumped out of the van, opened the back and got Slider's cage, and sat it on Nora's lap.

I couldn't believe it! I suppose Dr. Strann is a pushover for anybody who acts as crazy about snakes as Nora just did. What an act she puts on. I'd never be able to pull off anything like that. Girls sure get away with murder.

Nobody felt like talking, so it was a quiet ride going back. We only made one stop, for gas. Dr. Strann pulled up to a self-serve station, filled the tank, and went inside to pay.

Just as he was returning, Nora reached over and put Slider's cage down on the floor with the other cages.

When Dr. Strann slid in under the wheel, he looked over at Nora automatically.

"We're almost home," Nora told him, "so I put the cage back with the others."

Dr. Strann nodded absently. From the way he took off from the station, we could tell he was anxious to have this ride over with as quickly as possible.

When we got to the corner of my street, Nora suddenly asked Dr. Strann to stop.

"We can walk from here," she said. "The house is only a little way down. You must be in a hurry to get back to the zoo."

"Yes I am. "

Nora hopped out of the van almost before it came to a stop. I jumped out, too, ran around to the front of the van and grabbed my books and gym bag. Dr. Strann waved and zoomed off, leaving us standing on the corner, looking at each other.

"Okay," I said. "You're up to something. What's going on?"

"Open your gym bag," she urged me. "Not too much. Just enough so you can look inside."

When I just stood there, she snapped, "Will you just do what I tell you?"

So I zipped the bag open partway. My jaw dropped. "Are you crazy?" I yelled. "You can't steal Slider."

"I'm not stealing him, Harvey. I'm just borrowing him. I'll give him back."

"You bet you will. Dr. Strann will probably call as soon as he gets back to the zoo."

"He won't notice. You didn't notice the cage was empty, did you?" she asked.

"He'll notice sometime. Anyway" — I was mad about something else now — "why'd you stick him in my gym bag?"

"Don't you know anything?" she demanded. "How are we supposed to get Slider into the house? You think we can walk in just *carrying* him?"

"You want us to *sneak* him in? We'll never get away with that. They'll find out right away. Where would we keep him, anyway? We don't have his cage."

"You've got that little fish tank in your room that you don't use anymore. It's even got a good screen lid on it. It would be just right for Slider. Come on, Harvey," she pleaded. "What harm can it do? We just have to keep him hidden for a little while, just until Dr. Strann finds out and calls. You *like* Slider, don't you?" she asked, sounding anxious.

The way she said that reminded me of the way she spoke in the courtroom. So I agreed. I couldn't help it.

"It will be our secret," Nora said, her eyes shining. "Secrets are a lot of fun, aren't they?"

"Sure," I said.

How was I to know I'd just made the biggest mistake of my life?

# 8
# In which a snake is part of the scenery

I guess it was too much to expect that Nora and I would just be able to walk into the house and get Slider up to my room without seeing anyone. We purposely didn't go into the kitchen through the back door because it was late and we knew my mom would be preparing supper. So we went in through the front door, just like company, and ran smack into Mom and Aunt Mildred at the foot of the stairway.

"Nora!" My aunt rushed over and clutched my cousin as if Nora had just been rescued from a tribe of headshrinkers. "Your uncle Thor called us. My poor baby!"

Nora cringed. Who wouldn't? She's ten years old, for Pete's sake. And two inches taller than I am.

"Mildred," my mom said, releasing Nora from my aunt's iron grip, "let's not rehash all that right now. I'd like to get supper going, and I'll need your help."

Nora gave me a relieved look. If the two of them went into the kitchen, we'd be able to get Slider upstairs right away. And then Mom fixed us.

"Let me have your gym bag, Harvey. I have to put a wash through later, and your sneakers are a disgrace."

"My gym bag," I repeated hollowly.

"Wasn't I speaking the king's English?" Only one full day of my aunt and my mom was already turning snappish. She held out her hand. "Your gym bag, if you don't mind."

"I'll empty it, Aunt Joy," Nora suggested quickly. "You have so much to do. It's no trouble, honestly!"

Before my mom could react, Nora went racing off with my bag through the dining room, into the kitchen, and out to the little laundry room.

"I'll give her a hand," I said and took off after Nora. Behind me I could hear Aunt

Mildred saying in a pleased voice, "Isn't it wonderful how the two cousins get along with each other?"

Mom didn't answer, but her silence filled the room. She wasn't buying that at all.

Georgeann was in the kitchen making a salad. She doesn't just tear up lettuce and stuff; she makes a big production of it. She calls it expressing yourself. She had a cookbook propped open on the table to a fancy color photograph, and was following directions as if she'd be shot at dawn if she missed a single step.

Whenever she puts one of her salads on the table and we dig in, she winces. She's like an artist whose masterpiece is being destroyed by barbarians. I don't understand how anybody can get so emotional about lettuce.

"What's up?" Georgeann asked as I whizzed by, never taking her eye from her book.

I didn't answer and she wasn't interested.

In the laundry room, Nora had pulled my gym clothes and sneakers out of my bag and thrown them in the washer. Then she started to walk out of the room, still holding the bag.

"Hey! I always leave the bag on the shelf over the washer," I told her. "You'll just have to take Slider out."

"Then how will we get Slider upstairs without anyone seeing him?"

"We'll sneak him into the sunroom. We can go into the dining room from there," I explained, "and then you can take him upstairs."

Mom always complains about having so many doors — two doors in the dining room, one leading into the sunroom and the other into the kitchen; doors in the kitchen, one to the dining room, one to the outside world, one to the laundry room, one to the sunroom. Doors, doors, doors! But they sure make getting in and out awfully handy.

"We still have to get past Georgeann," Nora said, objecting.

"Georgeann is creating. You could float a battleship through there right now and she wouldn't see it."

Nora wasn't convinced, but she didn't know what else to do. So, holding Slider behind her back, she eased past Georgeann and opened the door to the sunroom. I moved right alongside her, screening her as much as I could.

"What's up?" Georgeann asked me again, studying the effect of tomatoes against the dark green of the spinach leaves.

"We just robbed a bank and we're going to divide the loot now," I said.

"Okay. Hand me the caraway seeds," she answered absent-mindedly.

"See?" I told Nora as I handed my sister the shaker.

We closed the door behind us quietly and tiptoed to the middle of the sunroom. Nora put her ear against the door that led to the dining room and listened hard.

"They just went into the kitchen," she reported after a minute.

"Quick. We can make it now," I whispered.

We were at one end of the dining room and had to cross the whole length of that long narrow area to get to the steps. We had just about made it as far as the table when we heard my mom's voice.

"You might as well set the table, Mildred."

At that very moment, my dad walked through the front door, shouting, "I'm home, dear."

We were boxed in.

"What'll we do?" Nora was in a panic. "We can't put Slider in any of the chest drawers. That's where the silverware is. And the tablecloths and napkins and stuff."

I had to think fast. I rolled my eyes and looked up at the light over the table, praying for an answer. And I had it!

I climbed up on one of the chairs. "Hand me Slider. Quick!"

Nora caught on right away. She handed Slider to me and watched silently as I stuck him up on the chandelier. It's made mostly of black wrought iron, all twisting and turning, with a lot of small shaded bulbs around the bottom.

Slider was so glad to be free he just naturally wound himself around the iron. Because he was mostly black, he blended right in.

I hardly had time to get down from the chair and push it back into place when Aunt Mildred came through one door and Dad came in from the hall. My aunt wanted an instant replay of our wild ride in the car. While she and my dad were talking, Nora and I set the table so fast, if it had been an Olympic sport we'd both have won gold medals. When my aunt finally turned around, she was amazed.

"Thor," she told my father, just bubbling over, "you wouldn't believe how marvelously these two are getting on."

My dad didn't believe it any more than my mom did, but he's a judge, and there was the evidence right in front of him, Nora and me working like a team. He just made a grunting sound and went into the living room to read his paper; Aunt Mildred went into the kitchen.

"Get Slider down," Nora ordered. "We can't leave him in the chandelier."

But I couldn't get him down. The traffic in that room was incredible, what with Georgeann in and out, Aunt Mildred fussing around, and Mom bringing in the soup bowls and bread and stuff. And then we all had to sit down at the table, and we were really trapped.

Nora and I tried desperately not to look up, but we couldn't help sneaking glances at the chandelier. Right in the middle of the meat course, when Mom was dishing out the stew, Slider wound his way down the fixture, slow and easy. Then he dropped part of his body clear and began to swing back and forth, like the pendulum in the grandfather clock in the hall. I was so scared he'd decide to drop down on the table, my toes curled.

Nora swallowed a mouthful and made awful choking noises. She had everybody's attention except mine. All I could do was stare helplessly at Slider. If he came down any lower, he'd be part of the stew.

Maybe Slider got the vibrations from my pounding heart, because he pulled himself up again and disappeared back into the chandelier. It was only just in time, too; Georgeann suddenly frowned, leaned back, and studied the overhead light suspiciously. Fortunately, Slider wasn't visible against the black wrought iron.

Georgeann sent me a puzzled look, stared at Nora for a long minute, then shrugged.

That supper had to be the longest meal in the world. Nora and I refused dessert, hoping the others would as well, but they didn't. When everyone was finally finished eating, Nora and I broke all records again clearing the table. We sure had our folks worried. Only Georgeann was relieved. Now she could talk on the phone to Hank without having my mom turn into an icicle because she wasn't helping with the dishes.

After a while, the grownups went into the living room to watch the evening news. Since there was the usual number of disasters to keep them occupied, Nora and I got Slider upstairs and into the fish tank without anyone spotting us.

I sank down to the floor, exhausted.

"We've got to give him back," I said. "I'm too young to die of shock."

Nora giggled. "I thought I'd die, too, when Slider was swinging back and forth over the table."

"I'm not kidding," I insisted. "How are we going to keep Slider a secret? We have to go to school. Somebody's going to find him."

"Today is Friday," Nora reminded me. "We don't have to go to school until Monday. We can hide him until then."

"And what happens on Monday?" I wanted to know.

"Oh, Monday." She waved her hand in the air. "That's still a long way off."

"Oh, yeah? Listen," I warned. "A lot can happen between now and then."

"Like what?"

"Like some kind of terrible disaster," I said. And I was right.

# 9
# In which a lady screams

I went downstairs again after a little while because I didn't feel comfortable in my room anymore, at least while Nora was using it. It just didn't feel the same.

For one thing, Nora took down all my baseball and football pictures and pennants and put up posters about saving whales and baby seals and the duck-billed platypus.

I had a measuring chart hanging on my closet door that showed how many inches I had grown, with lots of unmarked inches left to show how much taller I could expect to be.

I suppose Nora just couldn't resist it because she had marked off *her* height above mine. I reached over and yanked the chart off the door.

"This is kid stuff," I told her. "I don't need this chart anymore."

She didn't say anything, just gave me one of her smiles.

Nora had bumper stickers pasted on the door, too, that said things like I BRAKE FOR GO-RILLAS, and LIONS HAVE PRIDE and ZEBRAS LOOK GOOD IN STRIPES.

Dad says I'm suffering from invasion of privacy. I'll go along with that.

When I left, Nora was sitting up on my bed with the pillows piled high behind her back, reading about snakes in the encyclopedia.

I didn't see how Nora could act so relaxed. But since she promised to put the fish tank way in the back of the closet, where Slider would be well hidden, I went to bed that night feeling calmer than I had since my aunt and cousin came.

I stayed calm all through Saturday morning. Saturday afternoon wasn't too bad, either. My mom and Aunt Mildred went hunting for bargains in something they called a white sale, which turned out to be buying sheets and towels that were flowered and patterned and all different colors. Georgeann was at her ballet class. The only reason my sister takes ballet lessons is because she likes the way she looks in a leotard.

Dad was out mowing the lawn; Butch was stretched out on the porch supervising. That dog sure loves to watch people work.

I was in the sunroom sorting out my baseball cards when Nora came in carrying Slider.

"What do you think you're doing?" I yelled at her.

"Slider is bored. He needs a change of scenery. Besides, he has to have his exercise. We just can't keep him cooped up in the fish tank all the time. Dr. Strann wouldn't like it."

Just then the phone rang.

"I'll bet that's Dr. Strann now. You'd better get Slider back in the fish tank so he can pick him right up," I ordered.

Nora paid no attention, just curled Slider around her arm. "Slider didn't want to stay upstairs, did you, Slider?" she asked him, running a hand up and down his body.

"How do you know what he wants?"

"I can communicate with snakes," she said, sounding like her usual self.

The phone had stopped ringing by now.

"Well, communicate him back upstairs," I told her, and grabbed her arm.

Slider didn't like that at all. He unwound himself, slipped down to the floor, and got as far away from us as he could.

"Now look what you've done," Nora snapped at me.

I didn't stop to argue. "Find him! Suppose Dad comes in. Suppose he lets Butch in."

That got her moving.

We turned that sunroom practically upside down, but Slider had pulled a vanishing act.

"Maybe he's in the dining room," Nora suggested. "I left the door open when I came in here. He could have gone through real fast."

So we went into the dining room, dropping down on our hands and knees to peer under the table and chairs and the chest.

"What are you kids doing?" a voice asked, and there was my dad, mopping his brow even though it was cool outside, staring down at us.

"I lost my lucky coin." The words just seemed to pop out of Nora's mouth. "If I don't find it, a terrible tragedy will strike down all who live here."

I tried not to groan, but Dad was amused. "Is that a fact? Well then, you'd better find it, hadn't you?"

We could hear Butch scratching at the door. That dog thinks being by himself for twenty seconds is cruel and inhuman punishment.

"Don't let him in, Dad," I begged as he turned to go and open the door.

"Why not?" He half-turned back, surprised at my request.

"Why not?" I asked Nora under my breath. Everything was happening so quickly, I couldn't think.

Nora rushed to my rescue. "It's because Butch is depressed from spending too much time indoors. Aunt Joy wants him to stay out in the sun and cheer up. Oh, look." She jumped to her feet. "I found my lucky coin." She didn't show my dad anything, just shoved her hand into one of the pockets in her jeans.

"Good for you," Dad said, and escaped into the kitchen. We heard the water running from the faucet, the clinking of ice cubes in a glass, and then the back door being slammed shut.

"Butch is depressed from staying in the house," I started in a disgusted voice.

"There's Slider. He just went across the hall. Come on!"

We got there as fast as we could, but Slider was nowhere in sight.

"Where could he be?" Nora asked, beginning to look and sound frustrated.

"How should I know? I hope you're satisfied." I couldn't help rubbing it in. "He's getting plenty of exercise now."

You know what they say about finding a needle in a haystack. That would be a cinch compared to finding a snake in a room full of super hiding places.

"Where could he *be?*" Nora asked again, when we had turned over the last cushion and looked under the last chair in the room.

We heard the front door open, so we dived into chairs and tried to look as if we'd been sitting there having a quiet conversation. Georgeann came in, went past the living room, then doubled back.

"What are you two up to?" she asked, staring at us through narrowed eyes.

"How come you're always so suspicious?" I asked. "We're just resting . . ."

"Resting from what?" Georgeann wanted to know right away.

"Harvey lost his favorite baseball picture and we were looking for it." That was Nora, coming to my rescue again. "It's been signed personally by Reggie Anderson—"

"*Jackson,*" I said. "Jackson."

Georgeann came a little closer. "You have an autographed picture from Reggie Jackson? I didn't know that. Hank is a great fan of his. I'll help you look for it."

I shot my sister an irritated glance. "I thought Hank was wild about poetry. How comes he likes baseball?"

Georgeann shook her head at me. "Honestly, Harvey. You don't understand anything, do you?"

Just then my mom and Aunt Mildred came through the front door. Maybe "fell through" is a better description. They were exhausted. Aunt Mildred collapsed in the easy chair closest to her, almost knocking over the huge planter that sits right behind the chair. "I'll never get up again," she gasped. "Nora dear, take my packages upstairs, will you? I can't move."

"We could all use some coffee." Mom was already on her way to the kitchen, dropping her bundles on the dining room table.

Georgeann told nobody in particular, "I think I'll call Hank and tell him about the picture," and disappeared into the sunroom. We could hear Dad talking to Mom in the kitchen. He must have come in the back door. He really enjoys her company, I guess, or else he needed an excuse to stop mowing the lawn. Of course, Butch was with him. Trust him to be good old Johnny-on-the-spot when it comes to food.

Nora had run upstairs with the packages and was now back in the living room. She tried to persuade her mother to join the others in the kitchen.

Aunt Mildred waved her away. "In a little while, dear," she muttered. "I really must rest for a minute." She let her head drop back against the chair, closed her eyes, and in a few minutes, while Nora and I held our breaths, she dozed off, making a small snoring sound through her parted lips. Which was just as well, because Nora and I spotted Slider just then at the same time.

He had burrowed his way deep into the planter. Now he was pushing his head up, peering around, as if he was testing to see if it was safe to come up for air.

"Grab him," Nora whispered. "I'll stand in front of my mom. If she wakes up, I'll keep her occupied."

Slider looked as if he'd like to visit Aunt Mildred because he was beginning to move toward her, lifting his head and weaving back and forth a little way behind her. I yanked Slider up and out. Then I went tearing up the steps three at a time, with Nora pounding behind me. I was heading for my room, but Nora had a different idea.

"He's filthy, Harvey. We'll have to wash him."

"You can't wash a *snake*," I tried to tell her, but she interrupted.

"Snakes love water. It says so in the encyclopedia. Besides, he's covered with dirt."

She didn't wait to hear any more objections, just went straight to the bathroom and ran water into the tub. She kept on talking, though. "Listen, they're all going to have coffee. They're tired, so they'll be sitting at the table practically forever. And Georgeann hardly ever comes upstairs anymore."

So against my better judgment I put Slider in the tub. Pretty soon he was having a high old time. I went and got an old red rubber ball Butch plays with once in a while and tossed it into the tub. Slider kept swooshing around it, making it bob up and down like a toy sailboat.

I watched Nora playing with Slider, giggling and splashing. And I suddenly realized something. Playing with a pet, even a snake, made a big difference in Nora. It was the first time I ever saw her so happy and relaxed. She wasn't doing anything weird or nutty. She was just having fun.

I was still nervous, though. I went to the head of the steps to listen. When I turned my head back toward the bathroom, I saw Nora slip out and head for my room.

I just took it for granted that she had Slider with her. I breathed a deep sigh of relief, but I sighed too soon. Aunt Mildred was coming up the steps, heading for the bathroom. She'd no sooner closed the door when she flung it open again. She came staggering out, clutching at her chest, and gurgled in a strangled voice, "Snake! There's a snake in the bathtub!"

Then she went to the head of the steps and screamed her head off.

# 10
# In which a cold nose brings on a crisis

The whole family, including Butch, got up the steps in a split second. Aunt Mildred pointed to the bathroom.

"There's a snake in the tub," she gasped.

"Get her back to her room," Dad commanded. So Mom and Georgeann led her away. Meanwhile Dad tore into the bathroom. He came out as fast as he'd gone in and asked me in a sharp voice, "All right, Harvey. What do you know about this?"

I didn't have any choice, so I told him everything. I don't know why, but I didn't mention Nora at all. When she sent me a grateful glance, I felt very noble.

"I didn't think you'd let me bring a snake

into the house," I finished. "But Slider is really a good pet, Dad. He's harmless."

"I'll go get him out of the tub," Nora offered.

"It's too late, Nora. He's gone."

"Gone?" Nora took a deep breath. "Well, she scared him, screaming like that," she said in Slider's defense. "Snakes are very sensitive to vibrations."

Dad kept his voice low. "Never mind all that. The harm's been done. We just have to find him quickly now. We don't want to alarm — "

He broke off when he realized that my mom and Georgeann were standing behind him, drinking in the whole conversation.

Mom whispered, "Shhh. I made her slip off her dress and stockings and shoes so she could relax. For heaven's sake, Thor, don't let her suspect anything. She thinks you've captured the snake by now." Mom frowned. She'd missed part of my explanation. "I don't understand. What's a snake doing in the tub, anyway?"

"He's not there anymore," Nora said.

We heard a sudden gasp. Aunt Mildred had come up behind us. She was standing there in her slip, her legs and feet bare, holding a shaking hand against her mouth.

"The snake is loose. Don't bother to deny it. I heard every word."

"Mildred, go back to bed. Nora and Harvey will take you to your room. Joy, you and Georgeann start searching."

Aunt Mildred put one hand on my shoulder and the other hand on Nora's and the three of us staggered back down the hall.

When my aunt got as far as her bed, she stopped. "That creature could be under there right this minute," she cried. She wasn't taking any chances. She plopped down on the floor. And exactly at the moment my aunt turned her back, Butch, who'd been standing in the doorway watching us with a puzzled look, came all the way in. He stopped behind Aunt Mildred and nudged her on the leg with his cold, damp nose.

Aunt Mildred screeched, "The snake bit me," and fainted.

Butch was gone and hiding by the time Dad and then the others came racing in.

"What happened?" Dad yelled.

"Aunt Mildred said the snake bit her," I started to explain, "but . . ."

My dad didn't wait to hear any more. He was on the phone and calling for an ambulance while my mom and sister stood there looking dazed.

Nora gave me her big owlish stare. She was scared.

I was, too.

# 11

# In which everyone has a terrible day

Aren't paramedics terrific, the way they come in and take charge? They've got all kinds of strange equipment; they sure know how to use it, too.

There were two of them. They talked in a cheerful kind of way, I suppose to make everybody feel that things weren't as bad as they seemed.

I sorted them out after a while. Joe was the one with dark hair and eyes, a serious expression, and the quietest voice I ever heard. The other one, Rick, had blond hair and hazel eyes and teeth so white you had to shield your eyes from the glare when he smiled.

"She said she was bitten by a snake," my mom told Joe.

"A *snake?*" he repeated, as if he hadn't heard the word right.

My dad said impatiently, "Let's not get into details now. We're not sure, but I urge you anyway to examine her quickly for a snake bite."

Rick shrugged. "Whatever you say, sir." But he rolled his eyes at Joe and shook his head.

"Is she going to be all right?" Nora whispered.

Rich winked at her. "Now don't you worry, little lady. We're going to take good care of her. Snake bite and all," he added with a grin.

"Her vital signs are strong," Joe said after a few minutes. "We can't find anything that looks like a snake bite. She just seems to be suffering from shock, but we should take her to the hospital for a checkup."

Dad nodded.

Joe and Rick placed my aunt on the stretcher and were ready to carry her downstairs.

"We'll follow in our car," Mom said. She ran to her room to get her bag; Dad followed to get his wallet and car keys. Georgeann tore into the bathroom. She always has to go to the bathroom when she feels nervous or tense.

Nora and I fell in behind Joe and Rick carrying my aunt on the stretcher. As we all started down the steps, Rick, who was carrying the front end of the stretcher, stopped dead so suddenly that Joe got mad.

"What's the matter with you? I almost dropped the stretcher." It was the first time Joe had raised his voice since he had come in the front door.

Rick answered in a strangled voice, "There's a rattlesnake on the steps."

"Are you crazy?" Joe peered past his end of the stretcher.

"Slider!" Nora yelled joyfully.

I guess poor old Slider thought he was being attacked, because he raised his head, fanned the skin out around his neck, and hissed at Rick.

Rick was so startled, he dropped his end of the stretcher. My aunt fell out, began tumbling down the steps, and knocked Rick down with her.

Slider turned around and slid away as fast as he could move.

The noise brought Mom and Dad and Georgeann down the steps in a hurry.

"Mildred!" Mom gasped.

"What have you done to my sister?" Dad demanded, his face getting redder by the minute.

My aunt was huddled at the bottom of the steps, clutching her leg and moaning.

Rick was sprawled out beside her, holding his right arm in his left hand, his face whiter than his teeth. "My arm is broken," he said. "What kind of a house is this? There was a rattlesnake on the steps. A *rattlesnake!*"

He shook his head and ran his tongue over his lips. He was scared and didn't care who knew it.

"Slider is *not* a rattlesnake," Nora shouted. "He's only a harmless little hognose snake. You scared him," she added accusingly. "Now I have to try to find him again."

Nora went scooting off toward the kitchen. She must have been watching to see where Slider was heading when he left.

Rick shook his head again. "Harmless, she says. Get me out of this madhouse," he begged Joe.

Dad helped Joe put my aunt back on the stretcher; then he and Joe carried her out to the ambulance. Rick got in next to Joe, who was driving. My dad decided to stay close to my aunt.

Meanwhile, Georgeann was getting what Dad calls a delayed reaction. She whipped around and said, "This is all your fault, Harvey Willson. You and your snakes. You're responsible for this whole horrible snake disaster."

"Georgeann," Mom snapped, "we don't have time. We've got to leave this very minute."

Mom took Nora along, too. Before the three of them left, Nora, who had found Slider in the kitchen, handed him to me. She was so upset she didn't even stroke him.

I didn't want to go with them. Listen, I'd had a terrible day. I deserved all the peace and quiet I could get.

After everyone was gone, Butch and I went upstairs. I stuck Slider in the fish tank, making sure the lid was on tight. I had a feeling Slider was just as relieved as I was.

I stretched out on my own bed, with Butch beside me. There wasn't a sound in the whole house.

It was a great feeling.

# 12
# In which a dog finds heaven

The next morning my aunt took a taxi home from the hospital. Leaning on a cane, she came hobbling into the kitchen while we were starting breakfast. Mom had just filled a large platter with a dozen freshly baked cinnamon doughnuts, and the smell was driving me wild. She was about to bring the dish to the table when she saw my aunt, so she put it back on the counter and rushed over to help her.

"Mildred! We were supposed to pick you up tomorrow. What happened?"

"I signed myself out. I'm not sick. I was just suffering from shock. That's what Dr. Bogart told me. There's nothing physically wrong with me at all. Except for my ankle. And that's only a light sprain. I feel like such a fool."

She looked around, as if she were searching for something.

"If you're looking for the snake, Mildred," Dad said, "he's gone. Dr. Strann came by early this morning and picked him up."

"His assistant unloaded the van and forgot to mention the snake was missing. That's why it took Strann a while to check it out with us," Mom added helpfully.

I wasn't really interested. When I'm hungry, I'm a lot like Butch. I want to eat. So I said to my sister, "Georgeann, hand me the dough-nuts, will you?"

I would have gotten them myself, but I was wedged into a corner with my chair jammed against one of the cabinets. Our kitchen isn't built for six at the table.

"You have to eat your eggs first." She put a dish in front of me, leaning across Nora to get at me.

I picked up my fork and shoved whatever it was around. "What eggs? What's all this sloppy stuff on top?"

"This is French cuisine." She was furious. "Sloppy stuff! That just happens to be my own very special mustard and melted cheese sauce."

"Listen," I told her. "You want to be one of the great chefs of the world?, terrific. But practice on somebody else. I just want my eggs sunny side up. With ketchup."

"You know what you are, Harvey? You're a peasant!"

"I *like* them with ketchup."

"Give him the ketchup," Mom said. "You'll convert him some other time. Go on, Mildred," she urged my aunt.

Georgeann slammed the bottle down on the table. "He'd put ketchup on ice cream if we let him."

"Have some coffee, Mildred," Mom suggested. "There," she told my aunt when Georgeann came over with the life-giving cup. Mom must think coffee is the healer of all times because whenever there's a family crisis, she reaches for the percolator.

Aunt Mildred drank her coffee in one long gulp, took a deep breath, and plunged on with her story. "I did some serious thinking last night and this morning, after Dr. Bogart and I talked."

Dr. Bogart has been our family doctor forever.

Dad swallowed a sigh and sent a longing glance at the newspaper. There's nothing he enjoys more than a leisurely Sunday morning breakfast with the paper spread out and conversation with him kept to an absolute minimum. But this was his sister, and she was a guest in his house, so he said politely, "And did you come to some conclusion?"

"First, I want to apologize to all of you for getting so hysterical."

"It wasn't your fault," Nora said. "You were scared. You thought the snake bit you."

"Yes, I did. And I was terrified. And that's my problem. Dr. Bogart pointed out that I've never tried to control or overcome my fears, that I've always given in to them. He said I needed help."

"He's right, Mildred. We've discussed this before," Mom pointed out.

I'd finished my eggs and they weren't too bad. I still think, though, that eggs ought to look like eggs when you're eating them. "Georgeann," I said again, "will you hand me the doughnuts?"

"You haven't finished your sausage yet."

"Mom," I said, appealing to a higher court, "make her give me the doughnuts."

"Your aunt is talking. We don't interrupt when someone is talking," my mom answered.

Georgeann made a face at me and sat down. Just then I noticed Butch. Conversation doesn't interest him. He's a dog who likes to get down to basics — sleeping and eating. He gave Georgeann a few hard nudges, but she just pushed him away. It was time for Butch to act on his own. He inched his way to the counter, stood up with his paws clutching the edge, and took a deep sniff. A shiver of delight shook him. He stretched his neck, opened his mouth, and lifted one of the doughnuts delicately between his teeth.

"Georgeann," I said in alarm. "Listen. Butch is —"

She turned and practically snapped my head off. "Will you please let Aunt Mildred talk, for Pete's sake?"

Who could stop Aunt Mildred? She was carrying on as though she was on a winning streak.

"Dr. Bogart asked me if I'd ever thought of

the people around me — my husband and my daughter — or of the way I impose on all of you every year, whether it's convenient for you or not."

She left a little gap in her monologue, as if she expected my dad or mom to insist she wasn't imposing. They didn't say a word, just sat there waiting for her to continue.

I was still keeping an eye on Butch. He was on a winning streak, too. He had finished his doughnut. There was a dusting of powder all over his face to prove it.

I was the only one who could see what he was doing. My parents had their backs to him, and Nora and Georgeann were paying close attention to my aunt.

Butch stood up and helped himself to doughnut two. My aunt, meanwhile, was sailing along on a sea of words.

"Dr. Bogart said I've been yanking my child out of school year after year, shuttling her back and forth like a yo-yo across the country."

I had a quick vision of Nora flying up and down through the air on the end of a giant cord. I thought it was funny, and glanced over at Nora to see if she was smiling. But she

102

wasn't. She was giving her mother a dead serious look.

"I tried to tell him that Nora loves coming here when her daddy is gone—"

"No I don't. I *hate* it," Nora said.

"Why, Nora," my aunt began, but Nora didn't let her finish.

"You don't know how I feel about anything. You don't even take the trouble to find out."

My aunt was thunderstruck. "You've never spoken to me like this before," she said, staring at her daughter as if she'd suddenly become a stranger.

"I tried and tried. But you didn't want to listen. You *never* listen." Nora shrugged and looked down at the table. She was close to tears and fighting it.

I was practically struck dumb myself. I'd never considered even for a minute how Nora felt about coming here. But I supposed if my mom dragged me out of school in the middle of the year and pitched me into some strange school for a couple of months, I'd have a fit!

I'm used to my room and my house and my neighborhood and school and teachers and friends.

My aunt reached across the table and took Nora's hand in her own. "What have I done to you?" It sounded as if she was really asking herself that question. Nora didn't try to answer. And the rest of us just stayed out of the discussion. It was something my aunt and cousin had to settle between them.

Anyway, it was still hard for me to concentrate on their conversation because I was trying to keep count of the doughnuts. Number six was down and Butch was now working on number seven. His face was completely covered with cinnamon and sugar.

Mom would have a fit when she discovered what happened to the doughnuts, but meanwhile Butch was in dog heaven.

Then my aunt said something that really caught my attention.

"Would you like to go home, Nora? Now? Today?"

Nora stared at her, speechless.

"I mean it," my aunt insisted. "We can get a flight home today. I'm sure of it."

"What's the use?" Nora said. "You'll still be scared, won't you? What's going to be different?"

"I can't guarantee a miracle, Nora. Nobody changes overnight. But at least I'll be trying, I promise. And I will get help. I'll be making a start. Joy," my aunt said, "will you see what you can do about getting us a flight back? The quicker the better."

Mom reached up for the wall phone.

Nora's eyes began to brighten. "You mean it? You really mean it? We're going home?"

My aunt nodded firmly. Nora turned around to me. "We're going home," she said, as if I hadn't been sitting right there listening. "You can have your room back. I'm going upstairs to pack."

She left the room, as if her mother might change her mind if she stayed.

After a couple of minutes, Mom hung up the phone with a pleased smile. "You're booked on a late night flight, Mildred. Tonight."

My aunt gulped. "A *night* flight?" she asked faintly.

"Now, Mildred," Mom warned, "you've just made that child a promise. Let's finish breakfast. I have some delicious doughnuts. Georgeann, hand Aunt Mildred the platter."

At that moment Butch had the last wonderful doughnut in his teeth. With half of it still sticking out of his mouth, he looked as if he were grinning at us.

"You pig! You awful pig!" Georgeann shrieked.

Everyone was staring at Butch now. Mom surprised me by laughing, a contagious laugh that spread to everyone else right away. Even Aunt Mildred was giggling.

The air seemed clear of problems all at once; it was nice to see how relaxed everybody seemed.

"I'd better start packing," my aunt said.

As soon as I could get clear of the table I went upstairs. I decided I'd like to say good-bye to Nora when nobody else was around.

She was sitting on my bed with the crystal ball in her hand. When she saw me, she waved me in. Staring down into the ball, she whispered, "I see your future. I see you putting your baseball pictures back on the wall. I see my posters coming off the closet door."

I took the crystal ball out of her hand. "I can see what lies ahead, too. I see a kid with no more snakes in her future."

"No more Slider." She sighed. Then she grinned. "It was fun, wasn't it, Harvey? Tell the truth."

I had to grin back. "I wish I had a picture of Slider swinging down from the chandelier when we were eating supper. Nobody's ever going to believe it when I tell them."

Nora gave me a thoughtful look. She got up, walked over to me, and stuck her hand out.

"You're not so bad for a cousin, Harvey."

I gave her hand a quick shake and dropped it. It feels funny to shake hands with your own cousin.

"You're okay, too," I said. I was surprised when I realized that I meant it.

Dad and Mom drove Aunt Mildred and Nora to the airport that night. Georgeann and I stayed home. That gave my sister a chance to make a late night call to Hank. After all, she hadn't talked to him for at least an hour and a half.

I went upstairs and studied my room. I suppose I have it back for good now.

I was so tired I couldn't wait to hop into bed. But I couldn't fall asleep. I kept thinking about all the wild and exciting things that had happened when Nora was here. Now that everything is back to normal, I wonder if I'm going to miss my cousin Nora.

# About the Author

A natural-born storyteller, Eth Clifford has written many books for children and she admits that it is her ambition to "rival Scheherezade and tell one thousand and one stories." She has also written four books for adults and one of her stories was made into a TV special for NBC. *Harvey's Marvelous Monkey Mystery* and *The Dastardly Murder of Dirty Pete* are available in Minstrel Books.

**POCKET BOOKS PRESENTS** 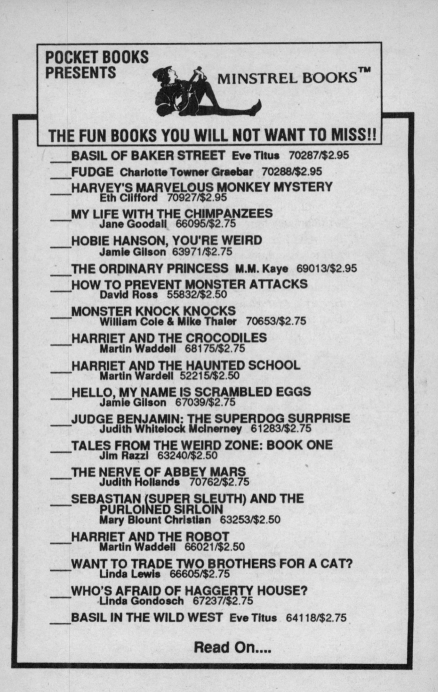 MINSTREL BOOKS™

# THE FUN BOOKS YOU WILL NOT WANT TO MISS!!

___ **BASIL OF BAKER STREET** Eve Titus 70287/$2.95

___ **FUDGE** Charlotte Towner Graebar 70288/$2.95

___ **HARVEY'S MARVELOUS MONKEY MYSTERY**
Eth Clifford 70927/$2.95

___ **MY LIFE WITH THE CHIMPANZEES**
Jane Goodall 66095/$2.75

___ **HOBIE HANSON, YOU'RE WEIRD**
Jamie Gilson 63971/$2.75

___ **THE ORDINARY PRINCESS** M.M. Kaye 69013/$2.95

___ **HOW TO PREVENT MONSTER ATTACKS**
David Ross 55832/$2.50

___ **MONSTER KNOCK KNOCKS**
William Cole & Mike Thaler 70653/$2.75

___ **HARRIET AND THE CROCODILES**
Martin Waddell 68175/$2.75

___ **HARRIET AND THE HAUNTED SCHOOL**
Martin Wardell 52215/$2.50

___ **HELLO, MY NAME IS SCRAMBLED EGGS**
Jamie Gilson 67039/$2.75

___ **JUDGE BENJAMIN: THE SUPERDOG SURPRISE**
Judith Whitelock McInerney 61283/$2.75

___ **TALES FROM THE WEIRD ZONE: BOOK ONE**
Jim Razzi 63240/$2.50

___ **THE NERVE OF ABBEY MARS**
Judith Hollands 70762/$2.75

___ **SEBASTIAN (SUPER SLEUTH) AND THE
PURLOINED SIRLOIN**
Mary Blount Christian 63253/$2.50

___ **HARRIET AND THE ROBOT**
Martin Waddell 66021/$2.50

___ **WANT TO TRADE TWO BROTHERS FOR A CAT?**
Linda Lewis 66605/$2.75

___ **WHO'S AFRAID OF HAGGERTY HOUSE?**
Linda Gondosch 67237/$2.75

___ **BASIL IN THE WILD WEST** Eve Titus 64118/$2.75

## Read On....

\_\_\_**THE DASTARDLY MURDER OF DIRTY PETE**
Eth Clifford  68859/$2.75

\_\_\_**ME, MY GOAT, AND MY SISTER'S WEDDING**
Stella Pevsner  66206/$2.75

\_\_\_**DANGER ON PANTHER PEAK**
Bill Marshall  70271/$2.95

\_\_\_**BOWSER THE BEAUTIFUL**
Judith Hollands  70488/$2.75

\_\_\_**THE MONSTER'S RING**
Bruce Colville  69389/$2.75

\_\_\_**KEVIN CORBETT EATS FLIES**
Patricia Hermes  69183/$2.95

\_\_\_**ROSY COLE'S GREAT AMERICAN GUILT CLUB**
Sheila Greenwald  70864/$2.75

\_\_\_**ROSY'S ROMANCE** Sheila Greenwald  70292/$2.75

\_\_\_**WRITE ON, ROSY!** Sheila Greenwald  68569/$2.75

\_\_\_**ME AND THE TERRIBLE TWO** Ellen Conford  68491/$2.75

\_\_\_**SNOT STEW** Bill Wallace  69335/$2.75

\_\_\_**WHO NEEDS A BRATTY BROTHER?**
Linda Gondosh  62777/$2.50

\_\_\_**FERRET IN THE BEDROOM, LIZARDS IN THE FRIDGE**
Bill Wallace  68009/$2.75

\_\_\_**THE CASE OF THE VISITING VAMPIRE**
Drew Stevenson  65732/$2.50

\_\_\_**THE WITCHES OF HOPPER STREET**
Linda Gondosch  64066/$2.50

\_\_\_**HARVEY THE BEER CAN KING** Jamie Gilson  67423/$2.50

\_\_\_**ALVIN WEBSTER'S SUREFIRE PLAN FOR SUCCESS
(AND HOW IT FAILED)** Sheila Greenwald  67239/$2.75

\_\_\_**THE KETCHUP SISTERS:
THE RESCUE OF THE RED-BLOODED LIBRARIAN**
Judith Hollands  66810/$2.75

\_\_\_**THE KETCHUP SISTERS:
THE SECRET OF THE HAUNTED DOGHOUSE**
Judith Hollands  66812/$2.75

**Simon & Schuster Mail Order Department MMM**
**200 Old Tappan Rd., Old Tappan, N.J. 07675**
Please send me the books I have checked above. I am enclosing $_____ (please add 75¢ to cover postage and handling for each order. N.Y.S. and N.Y.C. residents please add appropriate sales tax). Send check or money order—no cash or C.O.D.'s please. Allow up to six weeks for delivery. For purchases over $10.00 you may use VISA: card number, expiration date and customer signature must be included.

Name _____

Address _____

City _____ State/Zip _____

VISA Card No. _____ Exp. Date _____

Signature _____184-17

# POCKET BOOKS PRESENTS    MINSTREL BOOKS™

## THE FUN BOOKS YOU WILL NOT WANT TO MISS!!

____MY FRIEND THE VAMPIRE Angela Sommer–Bodenburg 55421/$2.50

____THE ORDINARY PRINCESS M.M. Kaye 69013/$2.95

____HOW TO PREVENT MONSTER ATTACKS David Ross 55832/$2.50

____HARVEY'S HORRIBLE SNAKE DISASTER Eth Clifford 70490/$2.75

____HARRIET AND THE CROCODILES Martin Waddell 68175/$2.75

____HELLO, MY NAME IS SCRAMBLED EGGS Jamie Gilson 67039/$2.75

____STAR KA'AT Andre Norton 60384/$2.50

____THE DASTARDLY MURDER OF DIRTY PETE Eth Clifford 68859/$2.75

____HARRIET AND THE HAUNTED SCHOOL Martin Waddell 52215/$2.50

____THE VAMPIRE MOVES IN Angela Sommer–Bodenburg 68177/$2.75

____ME, MY GOAT, AND MY SISTER'S WEDDING Stella Pevsner 66206/$2.75

____JUDGE BENJAMIN: THE SUPERDOG RESCUE
      Judith Whitelock McInerney 54202/$2.50

____HOBIE HANSON, YOU'RE WEIRD Jaime Gilson 63971/$2.75

____BOWSER THE BEAUTIFUL Judith Hollands 70488/$2.75

____MONSTER'S RING Bruce Colville 69389/$2.75

____KEVIN CORBETT EATS FLIES Patricia Hermes 69183/$2.95

____HARVEY'S MARVELOUS MONKEY MYSTERY Eth Clifford 70927/$2.95

____THE JOKE WAR Gene Inyart Namovicz 70489/$2.75

____HEADS, I WIN Patricia Hermes 67408/$2.75

____DO BANANAS CHEW GUM? Jamie Gilson 70926/$2.95

### Simon & Schuster  Mail Order Department  MMM
### 200 Old Tappan Rd., Old Tappan, N.J. 07675

Please send me the books I have checked above. I am enclosing $_____ (please add 75¢ to cover postage and handling for each order. N.Y.S. and N.Y.C. residents please add appropriate sales tax). Send check or money order--no cash or C.O.D.'s please. Allow up to six weeks for delivery. For purchases over $10.00 you may use VISA: card number, expiration date and customer signature must be included.

Name _____

Address _____

City _____ State/Zip _____

VISA Card No. _____ Exp. Date _____

Signature _____ 131-11

# Sports Illustrated

## AND ARCHWAY PAPERBACKS
### BRING YOU
## GREAT MOMENTS IN
## FOOTBALL AND BASEBALL

Sports Illustrated, America's most widely-read
sports magazine, and Archway Paperbacks have
joined forces to bring you some of the most exciting
and amazing moments in football and baseball.

## By BILL GUTMAN

☐ **GREAT MOMENTS IN PRO FOOTBALL**
   70969/$2.75

☐ **STRANGE AND AMAZING FOOTBALL STORIES**
   70716/$2.75

☐ **GREAT MOMENTS IN BASEBALL**
   67914/$2.75

☐ **STRANGE AND AMAZING BASEBALL STORIES**
   61125/$2.50

☐ **PRO FOOTBALL'S RECORD BREAKERS**
   68623/$2.75

☐ **BASEBALL'S RECORD BREAKERS**
   70217/$2.75

Sports Illustrated is a registered trademark of Time, Inc.

**Simon & Schuster, Mail Order Dept. SIA**
**200 Old Tappan Rd., Old Tappan, N.J. 07675**

Please send me the books I have checked above. I am enclosing $_____ (please add 75¢ to cover
postage and handling for each order. Please add appropriate local sales tax). Send check or money
order-no cash or C.O.D.'s please. Allow up to six weeks for delivery. For purchases over $10.00 you may
use VISA: card number, expiration date and customer signature must be included.

Name _____

Address _____

City _____ State/Zip _____

VISA Card No. _____ Exp. Date _____

Signature _____ 157-10

# CAMP Haunted HILLS

## by Bruce Coville

C ome join us at CAMP HAUNTED HILLS—the camp that promises to scare you silly!

CAMP HAUNTED HILLS is the brainchild of blockbuster movie director Gregory Stevens, a camp where kids can learn all about filmmaking, everything from special effects to directing and acting. But sometimes it's hard to tell where make-believe ends and reality starts.

Stuart's first summer at CAMP HAUNTED HILLS proves to be a great adventure—he is kidnapped by a family of sasquatch, chased by a mummy and trapped in a roomful of werewolves!

### *DON'T MISS* CAMP HAUNTED HILLS

☐ **CAMP HAUNTED HILLS: HOW I SURVIVED MY SUMMER VACATION** ................................ 68176/$2.75

☐ **CAMP HAUNTED HILLS: SOME OF MY BEST FRIENDS ARE MONSTERS** ................... 70652/$2.75

☐ **CAMP HAUNTED HILLS: THE DINOSAUR THAT FOLLOWED ME HOME** ................ 64750/$2.75

**MINSTREL BOOKS™**

---

**Simon & Schuster Mail Order Department CHH**
**200 Old Tappan Rd., Old Tappan, N.J. 07675**

Please send me the books I have checked above. I am enclosing $_____ (please add 75¢ to cover postage and handling for each order. Please add appropriate local sales tax). Send check or money order—no cash or C.O.D.'s please. Allow up to six weeks for delivery. For purchases over $10.00 you may use VISA: card number, expiration date and customer signature must be included.

Name _____

Address _____

City _____ State/Zip _____

VISA Card No. _____ Exp. Date _____

Signature _____ 240

**POCKET BOOKS PRESENTS**

MINSTREL BOOKS

## THE FUN BOOKS YOU WILL NOT WANT TO MISS!!

# MY LIFE

Minstrel Books introduces an exciting new series
**MY LIFE**—inspiring autobiographies of scientists, artists, astronauts, and many others.

Share the adventure and excitement of the world around us and those who have helped shape it in:

☐ **MY LIFE WITH THE CHIMPANZEES**
Jane Goodall .......................................66095/$2.75

☐ **MY LIFE AS AN ASTRONAUT**
Alan Bean .............................................70769/$2.95

☐ **MY LIFE AS A CARTOONIST**
Harvey Kurtzman .................................63453/$2.75

☐ **MY LIFE WITH THE DINOSAURS**
Stephen and Sylvia Czerkas ...............63454/$2.75

### * ILLUSTRATED WITH PHOTOGRAPHS

**Simon & Schuster Mail Order Dept. MYL**
**200 Old Tappan Rd., Old Tappan, N.J. 07675**

Please send me the books I have checked above. I am enclosing $_____ (please add 75¢ to cover postage and handling for each order. N.Y.S. and N.Y.C. residents please add appropriate sales tax). Send check or money order—no cash or C.O.D.'s please. Allow up to six weeks for delivery. For purchases over $10.00 you may use VISA: card number, expiration date and customer signature must be included.

Name _____

Address _____

City _____ State/Zip _____

VISA Card No. _____ Exp. Date _____

Signature _____ 223-05

## POCKET BOOKS PRESENTS

### MINSTREL BOOKS™

## THRILLS AND CHILLS FROM MINSTREL BOOKS

MINSTREL BOOKS brings you wonderfully wacky tales about what happens to Tony Noudleman's humdrum, ordinary life when he befriends a young vampire, called Rudolph.

Join the adventure as Tony and Rudolph get into one hair-raising, comical scrape after another when Rudolph moves into Tony's basement with his coffin, and introduces Tony to his mother Thelma the thirsty, his father Frederick the frightful, his brother Gregory the gruesome and his sister Anna the toothless—the family's sole milk drinker.

Don't miss these funny and scary tales of vampire adventures!

### By Angela Sommer-Bodenburg
### Illustrated by Amelie Glienke

| | |
|---|---|
| **MY FRIEND THE VAMPIRE** | 55421/$2.50 |
| **THE VAMPIRE MOVES IN** | 68177/$2.75 |
| **THE VAMPIRE TAKES A TRIP** | 64822/$2.50 |

**Simon & Schuster Mail Order Dept. TCF**
**200 Old Tappan Rd., Old Tappan, N.J. 07675**

Please send me the books I have checked above. I am enclosing $_____ (please add 75¢ to cover postage and handling for each order. N.Y.S. and N.Y.C. residents please add appropriate sales tax). Send check or money order--no cash or C.O.D.'s please. Allow up to six weeks for delivery. For purchases over $10.00 you may use VISA: card number, expiration date and customer signature must be included.

Name _____

Address _____

City _____ State/Zip _____

VISA Card No. _____ Exp. Date _____

Signature _____

227-01